HIDDEN PEOPLE

Do ever really know people?

Ben Barker

Attic Media

Attic
Media

ISBN-:9798879379891

Cover design by: Art Painter

Printed in the United States of America

"the only people for me are the mad ones, the ones who are mad to live, mad to talk, mad to be saved, desirous of everything at the same time, the ones who never yawn or say a commonplace thing, but burn, burn, burn like fabulous yellow roman candles exploding like spiders across the stars."

JACK KEROUAC

CONTENTS

INTRODUCTION

Hidden people exist throughout or society and history. People you never see, but who have a profound influence on the way the world operates. Think of the cleaners and waste operatives; maybe even the those in finance. Without them the world quickly grinds to a halt. One day I might write about them. Now think of the murderers and schemers. We might never know their names, despite having our world profoundly altered by them.

This book is about them. The ones who could be stood next to you while waiting for public transport. The person in the ATM que or the benefits office. They might never be known to you, yet may have an affect upon your life and the world you live in. This is the story of those hidden people.

PREFACE

Now enter a world outside the norms of society. One inhabited by a butcher, an axe wielding biker, a spy, a hired killer, terrorist and a telephone engineer haunted by his visions.

A world of hidden people.

PIES

"We've been invited to the meat awards!" Mike Orton shouted excitedly down his office phone to his wife. "We've been nominated for best regional organic product!"

"That's nice darling." Came the measured calm reply. "Does that mean a good night out?"

"Don't know, I would hardly call a presentation at the Regional Abattoir Butchery Business Industry Trade Society a good night out."

"Is that what RABBITS stands for? I just thought it was a joke!"

Three weeks later Mike had been forced to part with an increasingly large sum of money. There was the table for five, dresses for wife and his increasingly stunning - but demanding daughter, hair, makeup, new dinner suit and shoes. The costs seemed to outweigh the prestige of the award. Although considered a grumpy northerner at the best of times, he really did see taking their best friends Bob and Freya a complete waste of money. They were vegetarians – the RABBITS Awards didn't provide a vegetarian option being a meat industry event. Mike thought it rude that Bob and Freya had asked for their meals to come minus the meat, but the caterers had obliged. Mike could have booked for just him and Sam, but that would have meant sharing a table with a bunch of northern butchers, their robust wives and talking business the whole night. At least Bob and Freya were good company and daughter Sally just wanted an excuse to glam up – without the associated dangers of a school prom night.

Mike knew that by turning up to the event, he was in with a chance of leaving with a piece of engraved Perspex for the new shiny reception at his new shiny processing plant. Not to mention the publicity that would be generated in the local and trade press. This would put Orton Organic Products and Services firmly in public view. Orton Organics exceeded expectations, Mike collected three awards – best organic product, ethical business of the year and best marketing campaign for his 'OOPS it's organic!' A campaign that saw the cheeky little stickers spread across stores in the Northwest at exceptional speed and the company with growth to match.

During a much-needed toilet break Mike also made a new and unexpected contact. Just as he was zipping up his trousers a large friendly hand firmly slapped him on the back.
"Oops I hope that's organic!"
"One hundred percent!" Replied Mike.

It was the chair of the local football club congratulating Mike on so many awards.
"Are them pies as good as everyone says they are?"
"Yes." Mike was taken aback as he washed his hands. "Want to try one?"
"Sure, ones we serve at the town are a bloody disgrace. No meat and gravy like pissy engine oil."
"I can send some over."
"We'll never afford organic."
"I can do you a special recipe and cut the price. I can get a sample made up?"
With that, Mike agreed to get some to the ground by Friday and was invited to the match on Saturday along with Sam and daughter Sally. He didn't think they'd be interested and was shocked by Sally's enthusiasm.
"Course I want to go, there's some well fit lads on the side these

days. Do we get a visit to the dressing room?"

"I don't expect you mean fit as in their footballing ability?" Interrupted Sally, trying to be a good mother.

"Get real mum. Anyway, that young boy over there looks bored out of his brains. Do you think he'll run if I ask him to dance?"

Mike looked at the half frightened and slightly autistic son of a high street butcher.

"Run!" Mike said. "He's probably a train spotter and will shit himself."

"Well, it's just for tonight and not for life." Said Sally as she raised from her chair.

"Don't break his heart." Warned her mother.

Bob and Freya were diehard town fans, at least Bob was. Freya's loyalty was demanded by her husband who was keen to show off his trophy wife and status as a season ticket holder. They never missed a home game. Freya never complained and took a vague interest in the league stats. Her real passion was art, although her work had seldom been exhibited during the last ten years.

"Looks like we'll need a new shelf in reception for this lot." Said Mike admiring his collection of trophies'.

"Should make the place look less clinical." Advised Sam. "How about some new art works to cheer the place up. Some local rural scenes or something."

"I could do you a mural." A soft whimper came from Freya.

Bob reminded her of her vegetarian commitment, while Freya bit back that she was only going to paint the walls and not eat a bloody cow. The ensuing dark silence from the friends could have easily silenced the band as it played poor covers of eighties chart hits.

"Freya, that would be lovely," Sam broke the cold grimaces. "Such a very kind offer. We'll meet for coffee and arrange something tomorrow."

Mike quickly realised it wasn't the painting Bob objected too, he was just jealous. While he froze in his plastic seat on Saturday;

Mike, Sam, Sally and the butcher's boy would be enjoying the game from the directors box with all the warmth that corporate hospitality could throw at them. Hospitality that Chairman Hebblethwaite hoped would get him a good deal on some organic pies. Bob was also jealous of his wife. Age had treated her well, she added sparkle to a conversation and rooms were known to have been lit up by her presence. He was also jealous of her talent. Bob could turn a deal and push the stock market in new directions with the swipe of a mouse, but was this a talent? Apart from making enough money to pay off their large mortgage and to retire at fifty, he had little else to show for his efforts. Many people wondered why Freya stuck with the ultimate inanimate man, loyalty was definitely one of her strong points.

"Do you think Freya will actually come up with the goods?" Mike asked his wife as they lay in bed recovering from the ravages of cheap prosecco. "Is she any good?"
"Amazing," said Sam. "Just Bob doesn't let her work much these days, she paints a lot of landscapes and they aren't her passion."
"Doesn't sound good for our reception." Mike began to worry.
"She'll be fine, she loves large works." Sam glowed. "Twelve-foot interlocking abstract portrait canvasses were her speciality at uni."
"Not much call for them around here?"
"No, but she sold plenty in London to corporate collectors, that's how she met Bob. At a sale."
"Why did she stop?"
"Well…." Began Sam. "Promise not to tell?"

The promise came lightly, and Sam explained how Freya would paint studies of her life models and then bring them to life in large interlocked canvasses. Freya's mood would merge into the soul of the painting and give it a fervour that took the art world by storm. She would often paint naked and give her spirit to the work, she would spend days working without a break. The gruelling work, passion and expectations of collectors exhausted her. Bob lacked support and compassion, this led her into the arms of her regular female model. A distance was broken, but it resulted in some of Freya's most expressive work.

Her best received piece of work was purchased by a pharmaceutical giant that specialised in women's medicine – contraception, gynaecological products, and cancer treatments. It dominated the glass atrium of their London offices and provided a striking statement that they cared about women, their health, and bodies. Such a statement reflected positively in their share price and the corporation was keen for Freya to produce scaled down works for their publicity and advertising campaigns.

Bob was not happy. He saw the work as a direct threat to all he had worked for and crawled to achieve. He analysed, projected, and invested; yet there was his wife who achieved over night all he hoped for and worked years to gain. Freya's bank balance exceeded six figures and Bob felt she needed reminding that it was Bob's finances that had allowed her to work without an income before becoming such a respected and sort after artist.

Bob threatened to break Freya when he saw the paintings and reasoned out what had happened. He lacked the passion to physically hurt Freya, they both knew that. Bob would do it financially and leave Freya without a penny to her name. Freya agreed to leave the art world and concentrate on being a wife and mother, but nature had other ideas and Bob went further into abstracting every penny from the world he despised.

Freya continued to work on landscapes of the area surrounding their new northern home. The works never contained the raw passion of her London paintings, and she considered them only fit for charity sales and the local WI exhibition.

"Nude painting?" Mike was mystified.

"Probably due to spending the summer holidays in the Black Forrest with her German grandmother." Speculated Sam. "You

know what the Germans are like."
"Tell me about it. I'm never going to the German sausage conference again." They both laughed and embraced.

Following the game on Saturday, Chairman Hebblethwaite was impressed by the pies. As they sat in corporate hospitality, Hebblethwaite was into his second beef and onion pie when he spat at Mike.
"These are bloody good, and for a wholesale price under three quid! Can we have a thousand for the next home game?"

Mike knew it could be done. Saturday night was spent on the phone, and he had the development team in the factory first thing Sunday morning. The bribe of free season tickets soon softened any reservations the team had about working on a Sunday. Even the aging women food techs saw the advantage of tickets as Christmas gifts for the men in their lives. By teatime they had the recipe and machine settings to get the pies rolling off the production line. They had two weeks to perfect the product and roll out the publicity that would accompany the pies to their new spiritual home. Following the next home win the mayor had agreed to give the humble town pie the freedom of the borough. An honour only previously given to the local regiment and a local celebrity who later had it retracted upon his entry to HMP Gartree.

During that week Sam and Freya had also visited the factory and outlined Freya's vision for a large mural behind the reception desk. A painting of rolling hills, sunlit valleys, and a foreground of gleaming beasts. The idealised English countryside. Freya was to paint on a Saturday afternoon after shutdown when the town next played away. Mike would turn off the CCTV in reception and she could lock herself in without disturbance. Mike would be working in the adjacent open office and Freya could ring him on an extension if she needed him. Sam had Freya agreed to break from work every two hours.

Freya's naked painting became the elephant in the room, Mike was frightened to ask and Freya didn't mention it. When she unlocked the door for the first coffee, Freya was barefoot and wore a set of paint spattered overalls. They both knew, yet maintained their silence.

"Are these pies as good as everyone says they are?" Enquired Freya.

"I hope so," said Mike. "I'd offer you one, but being vegi.."

Freya cut him off. "I'd love one. Just don't tell Bob. He's the hard-core vegetarian, not me. Thanks to my Oma I was reared on German offal. Oh, some days I'd kill for a bratwurst!"

Mike fetched a pie from the cold store and heated it before returning to Freya, he also brought her some of the specially imported dried sausages that they were now stocking. Freya tucked in devouring the meat like a toddler who has just discovered chocolate.

"This is so good!"

"Vegetarians, I just don't get it." Mike puzzled. "What do they think will happen to all the animals if meat is banned?"

"Bob has all sorts of weird theories," said Freya through a partially full mouth. "Just like the ones that keep him investing his money in arms companies. You know some of your machines are made by companies he has investments in!"

Mike started to laugh.

"He won't eat meat but invests in its production?"

"He never questions where the money goes." Freya looked sad as she spoke. "He claims that it is the responsibility of the government not that of the investor. I just leave him in his room to do what he must and go and paint lovely scenes that I can remember from days gone by."

Freya's mood was glum when Mike helped her clear up at the end of the Saturday afternoon. It was as if she didn't want to return home to Bob in their soulless house. Even the arrival of Sam, Sally and her follower failed to raise Freya. Events were to turn much darker that evening. Sam took a hysterical call from Freya around 8pm. Something terrible had happened, she and Mike raced over to the luxury cottage Bob and Freya lived in.

Freya answered the door with her left eye already bruising. They found Bob prostrate on the kitchen floor in a pool of his own blood. Mike turned him over to find a boning knife in Bob's ribs just left of the sternum. Mike's knowledge of butchery told him that death was instant, nothing could have saved Bob.

"It will be alright." Reassured Sam. "We'll call the police, it was self-defence."

Freya started to cry once more and lent on Sam. She told them how Bob had seen her in the shower and saw paint on her breasts. He had accused her of having sex with Mike. Mike protested and his wife looked at him not in horror, but in a I know it's not true so be quiet sort of way.

"You are a lovely man Mike," said Freya. "But you are Sam's husband and there is now way..."

She began to cry once more as Sam comforted her and said she understood. Freya told Mike and Sam of the argument that followed and Bob going to sulk in his room amongst his screens. Freya had gone to the kitchen to comfort eat upon some of the sausage that Mike had given her earlier, as she cut a slice Bob walked in. He was enraged at the sight of Freya eating meat, not just meat, but meat from Mike. He punched her and twenty years of anger and frustration burst from her as she stabbed him straight through the heart. Bob fell to floor and Freya watched him fade and die.

"I felt no remorse." Freya said softly. "I had slain a monster."

Mike's mind raced, he was in cold calculating business mode. He knew that a knife through the heart would be interpreted as calculated, this wasn't a blind slash to defend or an unlucky cut to an artery. This was a direct intention to kill. That's the twist a good prosecutor would put on events. Everyone in the room that night would be under suspicion of having played a part in the murder. Sam believed Freya saying that nothing had happened between her and Mike, but the court and the tabloids would not believe Mike had been the perfect gentleman while Freya painted naked in the next room.

"We can't call the police!" Mike broke the engulfing silence. "We must simply make Bob disappear."
He explained his reasons and they all agreed that was the best way. They bungled Bob's body into the boot of Bob's car, the car that Mike would take Bob to the factory in. Then if there was an investigation, Bob's blood and DNA would only appear in Bob's car - the place it should legitimately appear. Mike would use his butchery skills and knowledge of meat processing to make sure Bob left the factory in such small pieces he would never be found. He didn't mention to Sam and Freya that he would probably feed the resulting mince to some nearby pigs.

Mike backed the car into the loading bay and began trying to lift the body out. He felt like a bucket of cold water had been poured over him as a heavy hand dropped on his shoulder.
"Hello boss. Want a hand?"
Shit it was Zoran! What was he doing there? Mike didn't know what to do.
"What the fuck!" Shouted Mike. "What are you doing here at this time of night?"
"Deep clean. Much overtime." Zoran sounded cheery. "You do this every Saturday night?"
"What?"
"Bring in bodies for the chopping up!"
Mike was horrified. His Serbian machine cleaner thought he was some sort of psychopath that went and killed someone every Saturday night just for fun.
"No, I don't! This is a one off!" Mike started to rationalise. "Go on Zoran, go and call the police."
"Why?"
Mike was incredulous. "You've just caught your boss hauling a body out of a car in the loading bay of a meat processing factory.

Isn't that illegal in any country?"

"Maybe," laughed Zoran. "I do much worse things with Bosnians. Anyway, I would like to keep my job. You are a good boss and I need to pay for my mother to have an operation. Calling the police would ruin all that. Need a hand with this poor fucker?"

As they lifted Bob out Zoran noticed the knife.

"You do good." Zoran sucked his lips. "Straight through heart, good kill. You once in the army?"

"No it wasn't me," protested Mike.

"Then you get rid for special friend?"

Mike told Zoran to shut up and they dumped Bob onto a trolley. Zoran laughed and said he would get the cutting room ready. Within an hour Bob was disembowelled, jointed and no longer resembled Bob.

"I'll crush and mince his head." Said Zoran.

Mike was about to question his motives, when Zoran explained this was the most difficult part to get rid of and the easiest to identify. Zoran made a good job and returned with a bag of mince meat and bone. They discussed what to do with the remainder of the now jointed Bob. It was Zoran who reached the conclusion first, Mike couldn't disagree with him. Any bit that couldn't be butchered such as bones etc would be ground and sent with the blood and bone to the organic fertiliser company that collected every Monday. The rest would be butchered for disposal. Then Zoran would spend Sunday giving the plant such a deep clean that the police would never find any evidence. The health inspector would see the factory as a shining example of how the meat industry should be run.

They also agreed that Zoran should disappear for a while. He would take Bob's car to the airport and leave it in the long stay and fly home. The police would eventually find the car and assume Bob had left the country. Bob called Sam, she was horrified, but knew it was the only way to protect Freya. They also managed to scrape together around £10000 in cash between them. This came from a slush fund Bob kept in a safe at home for emergencies and the petty cash Mike kept at the factory for paying farmers and the smaller suppliers. He knew he could repay it with savings the following week and Freya would be keen to assist with the expense of disposing of her husband.

Freya reported Bob missing on Monday, after the usual questions about how long he had been missing the police eventually believed he was missing. It was Wednesday before Bob's car was found at the nearest airport. CCTV footage only showed a man in a hoodie and sunglasses walk from the car into the terminal building. The cameras lost him in the toilets of terminal three. He's good thought Mike, he knew that Zoran was flying from terminal two. He'd only gone to terminal three to change his clothes. When the police finally checked Bob's accounts and saw the large movement of funds and £10000 cash withdrawal, they assumed he'd fled to avoid tax or had been laundering money and needed to leave the country.

Mike, Sam and Freya were questioned, but without the fervour they had expected. Dodgy husband legs it aboard and leaves his gorgeous wife to face the music was satisfactory enough explanation and meant the whole case could be handed over to a HMRC. This saved police time, it also saved several detectives who had enjoyed a long and undistinguished career having to put in too much effort before retirement.

Mike, Sam, Freya, Sally and her not boyfriend all went together to the next home game and took up residence in the directors box. Mike warned them not to eat anything made of meat at the game. Sally protested and her mother explained that her father had his reasons – these were match day pies and not the same standard as the ones supplied to shops. To ensure her silence on the matter, and in order to avoid an argument; Sam offered to buy her daughter a new phone.

"Bloody great these pies!" Exclaimed Chairman Hebblethwaite as he returned to his seat after the halftime break. "I reckon it's the pies that keep us going. They've put some fire in the squad. Not had results like this for years. You know some cheeky bugger on telly has nicknamed us the Pie Munchers?"

As they watched the game Freya and Sam both hugged Mike for warmth.
"Bob would have liked to have been here." Remarked Freya.
"Perhaps he is, just for today." Mike replied. "Each fan will share in a little bit of Bob."
"You didn't?" Sam quietly snapped.
"Had to put him somewhere. Where else would have he wanted to have been put to rest?"
Sam looked at Mike knowingly before replying through a smirk.
"OOPS I hope he's organic!"

LEGEND OF THE AXE

Axe pulled up, dismounted his motorbike, and walked into phone booth that sat along an uneasy highway heading south. He was tempted to make the call collect, but he knew the town's sheriff department wouldn't take the call. It would also let them know where he was heading in from and this was one journey that people of Hades County needed him to make alive.

"Hades town sheriff's office, how may I help you?" shrilled a high-pitched aging southern drawl.
"Amy! Shut up and put Hank on the line." Growled Axe.
"No need to be im-pol-ite," she snarled back. Amy covered the receiver with her hand.
"Hank, it's him." As she handed over the handset.

"Listen 'ere boy," yelled Hank, "if you lay one foot of your sorry ass in my jurisdiction yo'll not see morrow!"
"It's ten years and a day." Said Axe gracefully.
"My deputy's not Sir fuckin Gwain and yor no green knight."
"You and the Klan set this one up, not me Hank." Axe took a long pause. "Either we settle our way, or my next call is to some lily-livered journalist in Washington. Your call Hank."
"Okay," Hank sounded breathless, as if he'd suddenly been punched in the guts. "South Stix Bridge at midnight, come off the interstate from the south of the county and head north to the

bridge. We'll be driving down from the north. Yo' two'll fight it out in the middle of the bridge."

The line went dead, and Axe could smell the set up. Hank knew his arrangements far too well; he had probably organised a welcome to ensure Axe never made it to the rotting old girder bridge that was the southern entrance to Hades. He left the phone booth, took off his t-shit and stuffed it into a battered bag on the back of a battered Harley. He carefully took out a worn denim waistcoat that had once been a jacket. A jacket that had seen so many battles its arms were lost long ago. Axe put it on and once more the colours of the Prophets of Hades Motorcycle Club hit the road.

Axe headed south remembering the Prophets. Matthew, Mark, Luke and John; all from Hades. The others came later as the club grew in notoriety and statue. It wasn't part of the great network of biker clubs, it was no chapter to a great corporation, no part of a lost 1% that now had a website and sold merchandise. The Prophets were fully independent, that not only scared people, but it also created enemies. Axe was the last of the few. He was the first white Prophet and was invited to join after slugging a state trooper in Arizona. A trooper who'd stopped John for one reason or another, mainly for just being black and in the wrong place, the wrong place being his stretch of road. Axe even went to Hades with the Prophets and lived with Martha, Luke's sister for three years. "Lived" being what he did in between trips across the US. It had been ten years since Axe was ran out of town, now he was heading back to close the matter.

Having white skin, Axe was beaten and taken from town and left to die by the side of the road. The other Prophets were lynched, and their bodies left to rot from a tree for five days as a warning to those who challenged the order of the white power that ran the town. The Prophets women were taken to a barn out of town and after their suffering was complete the barn was bulldozed. It was Martha's father who rode out the next morning on Axe's bike to save his life. He also carried the warning from Sheriff Poulson not to return to town and a separate one from the local Wizard of White Knights requesting that if Axe lived, he should return in ten years and day to face the killer of his woman. Axe wanted to return to town kill him that day.

"You're in no state boy." Warned Marta's father. "They want you to return, it'll be biker tried to kill deputy sheriff. Come back in ten years, the town will have changed, and you may not be alone by then." Martha's father was more than a Prophet by colour. He had been detained before the killing started, but not harmed as Poulson knew that to harm Isaac would turn the whole town against him – whites included.

It was nightfall as Axe turned off the interstate, night was creeping in, but it was still early. Early meant Hank's deputies hadn't time to booby trap the road. They couldn't do it too far ahead because, because Axe still had friends in Hades who would be suspicious of the town's police and the Klan disappearing on mass. Axe even thought Hank might be a southern gentleman and allow him to get to the bridge unhindered. Axe found that he was wrong at his next stop.

Axe rode the Harley into the dirty parking lot of a dirty roadside bar. He could have ridden on, but he needed water. He saw the familiar pickup trucks outside and the familiar Wilton bothers playing pool as he entered the bar. Axe walked calmly to the bar and asked the aged bar tender for water. The Wilton boys carried on with their game as the bar tender handed Axe a plastic bottle of water and a glass.

"Yo' not going to the bridge to see the fight Ezra?" called one of the pool players.
"No point, can't see too good these days." Replied Ezra.
"He'll not make as far as the bridge, what'll yo' think biker?" Taunted another.
"Has little to say for a Prophet." Said the eldest brother walking towards the bar with a pool cue in his hand.

Axe saw him in the cracked mirror behind the bar and spun round delivering a low jab under elder Wilton's ribs. He exhaled and fell to the floor as his three younger brothers ran into attack.

Elbow-to-face, sole-of-foot-to-kneecap, thumb-into-eye, double-fists-into-temple, knee-hard-into-groin.

Blows rained from Axe into the Wiltons as they fell helpless to the floor.

It was then time to deliver his calling card. The signature that gave Axe his name. Axe collected his axe from the Harley. Legends had been spun about this axe. It was fabled to be a Saxon battle-axe. It was the legends that gave Axe his reputation and trash like the Wiltons the will to try and take it from him. In truth, the axe was merely a felling axe that Axe had machined to give it a better cutting action for fighting with. He'd only started using it to fight when a rival gang attacked him while camping out on a road trip. Till then the axe had merely been for cutting firewood. Axe quickly removed the heads of the dying Wilton boys and left a hundred bucks with the bartender to cover the mess and expense he faced. Axe left and rode on into the night.

Axe knew he was approaching the bridge as the number of people lining the road increased. Young and old, some with children and many who remembered the night the Klan decided to cleanse the town of The Prophets – the only defence the town had against corruption, bigotry, and prejudice. Axe was amazed and given hope by the number of white faces that appeared in the knots of people lining the south road. Hades was uniting. Bigots, the Klan and the police would all be on the north side of the bridge – the town side.

Axe stopped just before the road went out onto the bridge. Issac who was Martha's father, and the original town mechanic stood waiting for him and strolled purposefully out to meet him.

"Not too late to leave." He advised. "No one would think less of you for turning around."

"Needs to be finished." Replied Axe.

Hugs, handshakes, and fist bumps were the greetings of love Axe accepted as he walked out to the centre of the bridge. He was met by a steroid fuelled deputy stripped to the waist who had walked out from the other side. Axe could see the Sheriff Hank Poulson stood among his deputies and the newly deputised Klan's Men. They were armed with a variety of handguns, rifles and shotguns, but even these weapons would be no match for the anger they would meet should the forces of law and order try to pursue Axe.

There was no time for pleasantries as the deputy rushed to seize the moment. His physical strength was no match for the speed and agility of Axe. Even so, Axe prepared to receive the blows from his iron fists. The first blow landed squarely on Axe's raised and protective elbow. Axe knew that this had hurt as the deputy grimaced with pain and surprise. There was also a slow realisation in the deputy that the pain was essentially self-inflicted. He took a swinging punch at Axe that was so wide it gave Axe time to move and destroy his ankle. Axe had found a way into his body space and a well delivered punch to the neck felled the 250 pounds of Southern fried meat in one blow. Axe backed off to allow his opponent time to recover and withdraw; the hollering from the North side meant he was far more scared of losing face than facing Axe. He rose to his feet and attempted to throw another sluggish punch at Axe, it missed, and Axe's knee launched under his chest. Two more blows to head as he fell finished the matter. Within minutes Axe had cut off his head and rolled it towards the sheriff's side of the bridge. The receipt of the head was met with an angry silence that was eventually punctured by police sirens from the north and screams of joy from the south side. As Axe made his way back a large crowd that stormed northwards. It was time to elect a new sheriff as this one was unlikely to survive the night.

Axe shock hands with Martha's father who congratulated him and advised him to head home north through the mountains. He handed him an address.

"This is a bike shop in Atlanta, take the bike there. They'll fix it up and ship it north, cos I know that old engine needs some love. You take the Greyhound back to New York, that way you'll miss the state troopers who'll be out looking for a lone biker."

After what would be a last embrace Axe left and headed out on the road once more. The ride through the night was hard and Axe had to fight the nightmare of sleep that stalked him along the highway. By morning he found himself filling up with fuel at a small mountain gas station.

"Sheriff Hank Poulson has no friends in these hills." Said the aging owner as his impaired son pumped the gas.

"You heard the news?" Asked Axe.

"Sure did," replied the old man. "Sheriff survived the night, the state troopers are in town trying to restore order. Poulson is heading up here with a posse. We'll deliver him a real southern welcome if he sets foot in our lands."

"Stay out of it." Advised Axe. "The battle was for Hades."

"Like hell it was!" The old man shouted back the reply. "For years Poulson and his like have prevented ambulances leaving town and heading up here, that's why the boy's like he is and how we lost his Ma. We're outside his jurisdiction, but he supplies security for the mining companies that are trying to move us all out. You'll see you have friends here as you go up that road."

The old man refused payment and Axe feared what might happen as he headed home. Each bridge he crossed was guarded by locals who saluted Axe with their weapons as he passed, at each bend in the road Axe felt a hundred eyes were watching as he slowed the bike. Eventually he made Atlanta, news had even reached the city and Axe found him saluted by raised fists as he passed through the simmering suburbs. The sanctuary of the Greyhound that gave finally gave Axe peace and a time to sleep.

Days later Axe found himself sat at the counter of a New York diner with Officer Byrne as they drank their morning coffee.

"Looks like the cop killing biker has been out on the road again."

Byrne read loudly from his morning paper. "Time he was stopped and got the end he deserves."

"What happened this time." Asked Axe.

"Killed a Deputy Sheriff and three locals. Looks like he also incited the town to riot. Local Sheriff was killed when some hillbilly blew up his gas station with him and his kid in it."

"Probably a long running blood feud" Murmured Axe. "That'll be the end of it."

"Don't start getting all Dixie with me!" Joked Byrne. "A cop killer is a cop killer, and this one has been running for years."

Axe smiled as he stood, put on his cap, straightened his gun, and moved the baton on his belt.

"In which case we better be careful as we go to serve and protect the good people of this fair city." Officer Axel Van Houton he settled his bill and prepared to leave the diner with his partner Officer Byrne.

A DEEP COLD SLEEP

S oviet deep sleeper agent? Sounds glamorous? Believe me it isn't – especially since the Soviet Union ceased to exist. How did it happen? By accident and a number of unfortunate events conspiring to place me in the situation where I was suddenly wanted.

It was 1984 and I was a penniless sixth form student with no opportunity of a part-time job and without any chance of independent income. Having parents with a family business sounds romantic until you become the poor bugger who must spend their weekends and any spare time covering for parents or doing what my dad termed "... a nice little job." This usually meant shovelling crap - either real or metaphorical. For me the early eighties were more Auf Wiedersehen, Pet than champagne and Porsches. The boom time failed to progress further than the Watford Gap.

One night my mum found an advert in the local paper advertising for the Royal Observer Corps. This was a pseudo military outfit – volunteer civil servants in RAF uniform with the role of monitoring any nuclear attack on Britain. My mum pushed for this as she always fancied the idea of a son in RAF blue. My dad would have liked to have blocked it due to the sudden loss of barely paid labour, but given his ranting on compulsory military service for all teenagers, he was hardly in a position to argue.

The pay, hardly earth shattering and officially only expenses was £1.10 per hour plus travelling. Given that friends in supermarkets were only on 89p per hour this didn't seem too bad, plus travel allowance of about £3. The hours weren't great – two hours per week plus exercises. Now exercises were great, paid from the minute I signed into the building with scheduled sleep and rest breaks. As I was going to be on group headquarters staff with mess facilities and not a hole in the ground observation post with a bucket to shit in. Life in the Corps looked pretty good. Plus given dad's experience of national service he honestly believed if I didn't turn up for exercises the military police would come a collect me; he failed to realise this was only a voluntary service. The weekends on the calendar at home showed my rostering for exercises to be amazing full, it was also helped by my parents being so self-absorbed that they never checked with my friends parents to see where I was at weekends.

So, my recruitment into the Soviet intelligence service? Blame Thatcherite paranoia in Britain at the time. Everyone thought that Soviet tanks would sweep into Germany and then across Europe. US politicians told us it would be better to face nuclear annihilation that the yoke of communist servitude. That was alright for them thousands of miles away with Airforce One on standby to transport them to some far-flung safe zone that fallout hadn't reached. Servitude? The dole office seemed the only alternative in Britain. That was the main reason most of us went to sixth form, to avoid Youth Training Schemes and the benefit system. At least the Soviets promised a job for everyone.

Then one night the state of paranoia in the British military was brought home to me. At headquarters we had a pre-exercise briefing ahead of a real weekend 24-hour exercise. Much of it was the usual rubbish about the scenario that would be played out, pretty irrelevant to us locked in a bunker waiting for the fictional bombs to drop. Even then the sector controller would announce that selected targets held no resemblance to a perceived

Soviet strike and locations were selected at random. Really? Military headquarters at 8am, followed by military depots at 9am (COD Donnington our local military ordnance depot always appeared on my map), communications centres by 10am that included Criggion Radio Station – a low frequency submarine radio transmitter that everyone saw driving to Barmouth for bank holidays, or were they really trying to bomb the Dragon pub? Then the bombs got fewer and so did the status of targets.

During this preamble someone asked the question.
"In a real war how long would we get to man up headquarters? Would it just be the two-minute warning?"
"Indeed not!" Replied a full-time officer who carried far too much weight and an opinion of himself equally as large. "We anticipate a period of escalating tension, which is likely to follow a buildup of forces by both side along the East and West German frontier."
Hadn't I read about tank exercises in Germany being matched by similar in Poland, I just hoped they really didn't believe this shit.

"Senior figures anticipate a period of about three weeks before any nuclear weapons would first be used in the theatre of operation and then a strike towards civilian targets may follow. During this three-week period expect much activity will take place at home as Soviet Sleeper agents are activated and attempt to damage or destroy vital infrastructure installations. Structures that are vital to the maintenance of the civilian population. This would include water supplies, electricity and communications ...."

I couldn't believe that any of this was true or was he just telling the troops what they wanted to hear to boost morale and justify their roles. Being a Sleeper Agent running around the countryside with an AK47 and blowing stuff up sounded a better proposition than sitting in a bunker sticking plastic symbols on a map and learning to write backwards on the large transparent maps we worked behind.

"...Sleeper agents are likely to be aided by groups sympathetic to the Soviet cause and by members of the peace movement who may has been misguided into believing that a sustainable peace is possible. To that end the following part of the briefing has security restrictions, should not be written down and as you have all signed the official secrets act, should not be discussed outside of this room."

My dad would have loved this, signing the official secrets act was strange and mysterious to him and meant you had arrived in government circles. Little did he realize that posties signed it to stop them reading postcards from Blackpool and gossiping around the pub.

"... We believe that there may be an attempt to enter one or more observation posts during the forthcoming exercise. Therefore, a code word of ******* ******* code ***** is to be called by post controllers in the same way in which they would report a ****** code. Following this report, senior officers will take over from the controller and the police will respond to the affected post."

Wow! Something real at last. I still fancied the idea of Sleeper Agent; I wondered if they paid a retainer? I was to find out they did. Contacting the KGB was to become much simpler than I thought.
I found I could pick up Radio Moscow on an old valve radio that had shortwave radio reception. The station asked amateur radio enthusiasts to return QSL cards. These were simple a post card with signal strength information that would be returned to the broadcaster as an early form of quality control. I sent one with a message saying I had information and would like to meet and gave details of where and when. I put it in an envelope and assumed that all mail to Moscow would be opened, so gave no details where it was from. About a month later the 10pm news on Radio Moscow reported a large traffic jam on the M6 motorway. This was my signal to meet.

Meeting a real spy! I think I nearly passed out on the train going to the meeting. I didn't expect there to be anyone there or worse - the British police would be waiting for me. However, there on a bench outside St Philip's Cathedral was sat a thirty something not unattractive woman holding a copy the agreed three-day old broadsheet newspaper. She asked me for information, I told her the code words I knew. She looked straight ahead the whole time and didn't acknowledge my presence. She then named a hotel and room number for me to be at in one hour. Of course I kept the appointment.

What I didn't expect was the rough handling when I knocked the door. Gone was the pretty young spy, instead I was dragged inside, punched in the guts and sat in a chair. A gun was promptly produced and held at my head.
"Who are you?"
I gave my name.
"Why do you want to help us?"

I told them I was bored, needed the money, and was feed up with all the media hype that surrounded the Americans. I hated burger culture and felt there was another way. I felt I had blown it and was about to start blubbing knowing my life was over. Then to my surprise the large bear like men in the room started laughing and handed me a vodka. I was in, something had struck a chord with them, I don't know what and never will. Russians are wired up differently and their shared sense of comedy will always be a mystery to me.

I talked with their leader, he was interested enough to give me a post office savings book in an assumed name and promised there would be £50 a week in the account if I followed further instructions. This I did with upmost relish. I was one up on so many of my student friends and a fully-fledged Russian spy. I just had to keep my mouth shut.

Over the coming months I was able to photocopy the amendments to the Observer Corps manual that covered the new monitoring and communications equipment that came into operation. I was sent on letter drops, this usually meant getting a left luggage ticket or locker key in the post and phone call to say where to collect and take the contents. At one point I thought my phone was being bugged, hollow sound when listening to the dialling tone and last call played back if you pressed the two black buttons in the receiver cradle twice. We switched calls to an allotted time at the Sixth form public call box.

Then finally came the day when I was sent to be trained. A week in dingy former spa hotel in the Lake District. I had some difficulty convincing dad this was Observer Corps annual camp.
"Week on the piss more likely!" Was his outburst. Mum even tried to persuade me work for dad was more important, but I pulled the I volunteered for my country card. As look would have it, IRA activity also meant military personnel no longer travelled in uniform. This stopped parents' suspicions when I left wearing jeans.

Yes, I learnt how to shoot and handle explosives in some dire deserted quarry in the pouring rain, but I loved it. Now just to sink back into society and not spend the pay rise too quickly and arise suspicions. I was now a deep sleeper and didn't have to run around carrying letters and parcels. Any snippets from the Observer Corps were still greatly received. Life was good, then in 1989 it was all to come to an end.

The world and I had moved on. My university friends stood in wonder as the Berlin Wall fell. I stood in shock with the slow realisation the cash would dry up and I could be arrested as Eastern bloc records became available. Luckily our own secret service never did connect me, or at perhaps I was too small to bother with.
Thirty years later the Royal Observer Corps has been stood down and I'm stood attempting to deliver the lesson of my life to uninterested students, two members of senior management and an OFSTED inspector. The lesson was finally finished, and I

refused the offer of feedback.

"We believe it would be beneficial." Bleated a manager in a cheap suit who looked young enough to be my grandson.

"If I valued your opinion I would be prepared to listen." I told him and his open-mouthed colleague as I left the room. That night my old life would be brought out from a deep sleep, I was finished in education.

I managed to locate my old arms cash deep in the conifers of Cannock Chase. The contents all looked remarkably fresh. I removed the plastic explosive, timers, and detonators; before heading off for the climax of my teaching career. I wasn't going to kill anyone, but an awful lot of expensive cars wouldn't survive the night, the following morning the whole of my school's leadership and the OFSTED team would be using public transport.

Who would suspect a lowly history teacher? Not the police, they had many theories that were quite ridiculous. However, someone knew. During morning break my mobile rang, it never rang at school.

I slowly answered a quiet. "Hello."

"Knuts?"

"I like dry roasted."

"Would you like to try some?"

"Yes please, tonight?"

"6pm at our first meeting place." The phone went dead.

Sitting outside St Philip's was the same woman from thirty years ago, but now much older.

"A storage device was open yesterday, we would like to know if it was you?"

I knew it was no use to lie and admitted my crimes.

"Would you like to be reactivated?"

This shocked me and I manged to gurgle a reply.

"Good, then please appear at the offices of Shah Recruitment tomorrow and attend an interview for Eastern Gas." With that she left.

I didn't know whether to leave town or hand myself into the police, but I threw a sickie and attended the interview. Not really an interview, just a catch up on what I had been doing for thirty years. The KGB was now the SVR RF or GRU, but I would be working for a contractor and have a salaried job at a gas company. I would hold a recruitment and training position in the UK for eastern bloc immigrants. This sounded good, with contracts signed my next job was to resign from school.

"One bad lesson needn't result in immediate resignation." Said the head, but he had wasted his words and I was heading for the car park.

My Eastern Europeans were ready and keen learners, they appreciated my efforts to teach them English and culture. Quite what they have done with it I hate to think about, but I do occasionally see them appear as wanted for various crimes on the local news channel. Of course, the salary is far better than that in state education.

Then came the Ukrainian crisis. This wasn't the end, my students didn't appear to change, only their names and the colour of their passports were now different.

DRAGONFLY

R uth knew she was an expert in her field, a dedicated professional. There were not many contract providers working at her level. There were always the dedicated amateurs who were either dead or jailed, they were never in the topflight that demanded high fees. She knew of only three others who offered the same level of professional service as herself. They had never met, and an unspoken truce prevented them from crossing paths professionally. All Ruth's customers were checked by Frank – her old friend and mentor. Before taking this job, Ruth knew she would need to retire. She was nearing her fifteenth birthday, she could remain fit enough to carry on shooting for a long time. However, it was the other skills that needed to be sharp in order to keep her alive and out of jail.

Ruth laid out her shooting mat on the bracken and began to position herself.

Ruth loved her work. She quite liked her day job, but she really loved her weekend and evening job. This time it was an evening and weekend job she decided as she looked down the scope and through the illuminated crosshairs. She could see a party taking place at a large Surrey mansion and Ruth knew she was minutes away from earning a life altering sum of money or facing a life altering jail sentence. She took a long deep slow breath and began to search for her target.

He appeared with a tray and began playing the perfect host to his guests assembled by the pool. Well certainly the perfect host to the bikini clad females who endured to the chill of an English summer evening in order to pay their way in the world. The hardened professionals refused the packets from the tray in order to keep a clear head and avoid offering more than they were being paid for; while the students struggling to pay their tuition fees took whatever was going free. They would one day learn that nothing in life is free.

Ruth felt extremely lucky. A cold wet evening would have been a disaster, everyone one would have been inside. Two aspects of her job she hated – making shots through glass and short-range work that compromised her anonymity. Ruth settled down digging her elbows into the bed of bracken and soil that supported her body. She slowed her breathing, the rise and fall of the rifle barrel matching her body in perfect time. She raised her trigger hand to adjust the focus on the sight; she knew the range finder was set at infinity. She also knew that having to adjust the focus meant she was beyond the range of her previous target. She just hoped the estimations for elevation and windage would put the shot somewhere close to accurate. Ruth never called the target a victim, she never thought of her targets as victims. The very fact that someone was willing to have them killed usually meant the target was involved in something he or she shouldn't have been involved in. If he or she had been a good citizen, happy to have a social drink with friends or stay at home with loved ones; then he or she would never appear at the end of one of Ruth's barrels. Simplistic? So far true.

Ruth also knew from the adjustments she made to her sight, that the shot would be near to 1000 yards. Using an unsupported rifle, this would be a tall ask for most snipers. She regarded herself as a crafts person, an artisan and this shot would be more art than science. It was one reason for making it at night, the air would be more stable. There would be fewer rising thermals, no anabatic or katabatic wind; it was just harder to locate the target. Ruth could have used a variety of technology to help – night scopes (pain in the arse if the target was near a light), computer software and weather gadgets - all that added complications to the getaway. Ruth just enjoyed a craft approach to her work, good eyes and a sense of perception.

Ruth's worst fear as she lay in the undergrowth was getting discovered. There again, anyone who discovered her out on the heath past midnight was not there for the good of their health and she would have no problem sending him or her to another life. Ruth eased her finger back and took the trigger to its pre-fire position. She slowed her breathing to a pause as the target's head appeared in the sight. He was animated and kept moving up and down as he spoke. Knowing she had to abandon the shot and breath or get on and take it, Ruth eased back and fired. The barrel showed a slight jump as the bullet left and went on its course. Ruth stayed in position to follow through. She had learnt long ago never to move until the bullet hit the target, too many beginners move as they pull the trigger and miss. Also, there was the added advantage that if she did miss, there may be a chance of a second shot.

In the time it took the bullet to reach the target Ruth remembered her first stag - on a grey morning devoid of colour in a distant Scottish glen, with an old school friend and the family's gillie. He taught Ruth and her friend how to stalk and the importance of a clean kill. Lady Kilbreck (as she was to become) was one of only three people who knew of Ruth's second job. As plain Maggie she was Ruth's closet friend at school and would invite Ruth to her family home for holidays, at a time when Ruth's father was stationed too far away for her to make the long trip to the remaining reaches of the British Empire. Maggie knew of the abuse Ruth suffered from the headmaster at their boarding school – too far from home in a time before the internet, when a letter home could take weeks and might never reach the post office if the head had the slightest sniff of defamatory content. Maggie also knew that the head had been one of Ruth's targets, for he would never be a victim.

The time it took for the bullet to reach a target always felt longer than the actual time elapsed. The target stood up as the bullet drove into the front of his skull and delivered his brain to the bright whitewashed wall behind him. Ruth knew there was no need to wait around and began packing to leave. She left the spent cartridge in the rifle as she packed it, it being her favourite precision hunting rifle into a modified guitar gig bag. This was a semi ridged gig bag that was padded out to hold the rifle, it also meant if she was stopped while driving late at night; any misogynist police officers would accept her story of being a lone female musician on her way home after a late gig. Ruth made sexism work for her and placed her beyond suspicion. Female officers just admired her independence.

She also knew the client paying for tonight's work would become a wealthy widow and judging by her husband's performance it was money well spent. Ruth found it best not to enquire about her customers motives, but this one had left a very emotional message on Ruth's booking phone. Ruth was sure the world was a better place without him. Just like most of the people she had shot, blown up, stabbed or just throttled. Their passing would benefit the world and Ruth was safe in the knowledge she was making the world a better place.

Ruth had always loved shooting, there was something about it that enthralled her. It was like a form of magic – one small movement resulted in an event occurring a distance away. It would be an event that the person pulling the trigger was not involved in. She loved the skill, the control and the total focus of taking a shot. Whether it was a human, an animal she would later enjoy eating or just punching a hole in a piece of paper. She loved the totality of the art.

Ruth could see the clouds gathering overhead and felt the first drops of rain as she stood by her car and loaded her overalls and gloves into a medical disposal bag that would be incinerated courtesy of her local hospital. Leave one of those tied bags around a hospital just as visiting ended and it would be incinerated by the next morning. No trace of powder on her clothes or DNA left. That's why the police officers who had finally made the ballistic link between Ruth's targets had code named her the Dragonfly. Inspector Davies had once attended a wildlife talk and was shocked to learn Dragonflies can be the most brutal of killers, but never leave DNA - just like Ruth.

Inspector Davies had a ballistic link, he even knew the calibre and type of rifle she used, but he didn't know his assassin was female, he didn't know the true number of victims and he certainly hadn't got a clue where to find Ruth. He'd even had his team scour the internet for her and set up a sting operation. The result was he had to explain the loss of £10 000 of National Crime Agency money and no arrest. Ruth just went to ground and reappeared when she was ready. Her reputation was such that one text message via a public Wi-Fi on second-hand phone had re-established her back in the criminal underworld. A place where she could resume her bread and butter work of taking out rival drug lords for rival drug barons. Horrid work, but someone had to do it and Ruth thought it might as well be her. Scum paying for scum to be exterminated. She had no worries about the morality of the role; it was just a form of pest control.

Controlling the undesirable was why she murdered her former headmaster. She had to wait nearly ten years, but it was worth it. He had picked his victims with a cold calculating mind. He would carefully risk assess which girls would have difficulty in telling their families. Young girls with parents aboard and in the forces were least likely to cause trouble. In a pre-internet age, it could take weeks for a letter to be answered from far flung places such as Hong Kong. Also, when at home, the girls were so happy to be there they would not want to deliver bad news into the family home. Forces families also had the constant threat of Ulster hanging over them, children and parents alike only wanted to enjoy the short time they had together, and nothing would be done to spoil that time.

So, Malcom Sternfield continued his quest for sweet young flesh. He also had the school doctor to help make sure there were no unwanted pregnancies. It was the early poor fitment of an IUD coil that may have cost Ruth any chance of her own children, deprived of the opportunity to create life she now took pride in destroying it. Doctors were once all powerful and a letter to parents in distant lands saying their daughter had been suffering unusually heavy and painful menstruation generally resulted in permission to fit a coil. As parents did not want their precious daughters suffering unnecessarily and far from the comfort of home, the doctor and school nurse had free range to 'make safe' Malcom's girls.

Ruth had completed her degree and was studying for her master's when she returned to school for the only reunion she ever attended – a reunion party that was also Sternfield's retirement party. Ruth had planned her revenge down to the last detail. During the afternoon soiree she approached a lone Sternfield and thanked him for all that he had taught her. Not just the academic studies, but the extra curriculum activities that had helped her fully appreciate her time at university. Sternfield was hooked; Ruth didn't need to ask twice if she could see the inside of his study once more. They moved quickly into the study, and he locked the door as they entered.

Ruth sat him in the chair behind his large mahogany desk. She stood behind and unbuttoned his shirt. As she twisted his nipples, he unbuttoned his trousers – never one to be asked, he took his pleasure without waiting. Ruth removed a skipping rope from her bag and started to wind it around the high-backed chair and then around his neck. As he protested, she whispered in his ear that the lack of oxygen added to the orgasm – he was impressed. As Ruth encouraged him to masturbate for her, she wound the rope tighter and tighter until he started to make a gargling noise. As he came, the light of his life went out and Malcom Sternfield lay in his chair covered in his own depravity. A fitting end for an unfit human being thought Ruth.

She knew from old that he had a collection of pornography confiscated from teenage girls in the bottom drawer of his desk. Ruth opened the drawer and was in luck. Two special edition gay cowboy magazines. She lifted one out carefully using the latex gloves from her handbag, quickly opened it to the centre page spread and smeared Sternfields bodily fluid onto it.

Ruth congratulated herself as she removed the gloves and turned them in on themselves so that the any contaminants were safely contained inside the small bag made by the gloves. Removing gloves to contain contamination – one of the very few skills she learnt in the Officer training Corps (OTC) at university. Ruth hated the OTC and only joined because of family expectation, she knew if she hadn't joined she would never have met Marcus and she would never have been able to get hold of the weaponry that now gave her the tools of her trade. Marcus was of Afro-Caribbean descent, something Ruth's family appeared blind to. Her father was known as a forward-thinking officer, he only saw Marcus as a sensible young man who would make a good officer.

Ruth left the study via the French windows, just as she had when as a teenager she was sent back to prep after being abused by the very man that was meant to protect her and instil good virtue in the absence of her parents. Now he lay dead in the ferment of his own depravity. Ruth still had his accomplice - the school doctor to deal with, but she would wait so that there would be no connection between the sudden deaths.

Sternfield's death went better than expected. Letting the doctor have a few more years on earth also paid dividend. When Sternfield failed to return to the party, a search was conducted and several hours after his death the school porter finally broke down the headmaster's study door. Out of loyalty he prevented entry to all others until the police arrived. Another stroke of luck, Sternfield played golf with a number of local senior police officers, who in order to save Mrs. Sternfield any embarrassment made sure the scene was not photographed and Doctor Aster, the school doctor completed the death certificate. This was in the times before Shipman, a time when a doctor's word was final. All the doctor needed to do was add a few visits to the handwritten notes that formed his medical records and the whole incident was buried without further investigation – death by natural causes. Ruth had considered sending a message to Inspector Davies to exhume the body once she had retired but thought better of it as forensic technology had advanced considerably since Sternfield had departed for hell.

Ruth started the ignition and began the long drive home thinking of how she would spend her retirement. First, she had to clear up her life before leaving the country, trying to clear up her life was something she had been trying to achieve since that first advance by Sternfield when she was just 13 years old. Now she had the money to do so, her only regret was she wouldn't have Marcus there with her.

After university Marcus went on to become a career solider, with a family. Aster's crude medical technique had ruined the chance of family for Ruth, and she wasn't prepared to become an army wife like her mother; with her own aspirations limited to supporting her husband's career. Ruth and Marcus were natural friends at university, they even became lovers after Ruth's departure from the OTC. A departure hastened when a military training instructor attempted to humiliate Ruth, the only woman on parade that morning. Her response was a quick and accurate - a rifle butt slammed into his face resulting in two missing teeth, broken nose and a split palate. Ruth was asked to leave the OTC, if had not been for her father being a staff officer; Ruth may have faced serious charges.

Marcus persuaded Ruth to find a good martial arts instructor for her own protection. This she did in the form of Frank, a cage fighting scrap dealer from Liverpool who gave Ruth the edge that many women may lack when faced with the time of fight or flight. From their first meeting Ruth realised that she was going to have a career outside of the regular professions available to a young graduate.

Frank taught Ruth to harm without remorse, and he was the first person she ever told about Sternfield. Frank also helped Ruth plan Sternfield's demise while sitting in the quiet confines of his fighting cage - a sanctum where conversations remained and never left.

After the death of Sternfield, Frank also put Ruth in contact with her early clients who appreciated her refined methods of despatch. Frank became a mentor in criminal anonymity; it was he who taught Ruth how to make a mobile phone untraceable by buying it second hand for cash from a market trader and then using a SIM card purchased from similar - but far away from where the phone was bought. This technique she refined over the years to such an extent that she was now running her own website on the dark web using an untraceable laptop on public Wi-Fi.

Marcus had proved himself an invaluable friend. He forged a career as an army planning officer where his logistical skills were largely wasted and was often passed over for promotion as white privileged officers fulfilled their families righteous expectations. Supplying Ruth with guns and ammunition was done more for the challenge than the money she insisted on paying him. For the Surrey job he had wanted her to have a military sniper rifle, due to its long effective range – as proved by Craig Harrison's record breaking shot in Afghanistan. Ruth found the AI rifle too heavy and already fallen in love with the lighter sports rifle made in the US. The rifle she had used while on a hunting holiday in the US. Marcus loved a challenge and managed to import one for military testing and pass it on to Ruth, he really was a genius in Ruth's eyes.

With weapons supplied by Marcus and an expanding client list from Frank, Ruth gained a reputation for quick and swift doorstep executions and knee capping. The Manchester drug scene became Ruth's Sunday morning place of work, during the week she taught French and Spanish to ungrateful teenagers in a comprehensive school. This gave Ruth a legitimate income and prevented the tax authorities becoming interested in her affairs as Ruth was a legitimate taxpayer. As the years progressed, she cut her hours and diverted her illegal gains to a numbered Swiss bank account and crypto currencies. Ruth was becoming rich, but she was lonely. Eventually she purchased a cottage in a small Alpujurra village in the south of Spain where she could eventually escape to and become part of village life.

Two years after Sternfield, Ruth was to complete her masterpiece of waste disposal. She went after Aster - the school doctor. Fate meant that Ruth's planned doorstep shooting didn't happen due to the doctor taking city break with his wife. This also meant Ruth had time and a free hand to plan something more fitting, a deep burning pain that would haunt him in the last moments of his life.

The doctor's house was a large 1930s villa well screened from prying eyes by Leylandii. His large saloon car was parked on the drive, a make of car that every teenager knew could be opened with half a tennis ball pressed against the driver's door lock. Once in the car Ruth pierced the fuel injection pipe to give a fine spray of petrol across the exhaust manifold - the lack of run-on valve on that particular model had been implicated in several motorway fires. Two years later and this option would not have been available to the would-be car bomber. She then ran two wires from the ignition coil, one to the fuse on the central locking system and one connected to a piece of wire wool earthed to the exhaust manifold. Ruth then packed the engine bay with agricultural fertiliser and carefully spread more fertiliser in the car under the floor mats and in the boot.

Ruth watched as the doctor kissed his wife good-bye on a bright Monday morning. As he turned the ignition key, the fuse blew on the vacuum locking system which then defaulted to lock. The engine fired igniting the engine bay and the doctor was trapped in a burning car. Ruth remembers the look on his face as she waved him good-bye. Minutes later the car exploded into a fireball that hit the front door of his house door blowing his wife back into the house. Ruth didn't wait for the fire brigade to arrive. His scream of terror was her music of delight.

The drive down the dark roads of Surrey felt interminable as Ruth headed for the M25 and the long drive home. She arrived at her rented industrial unit on the outskirts of town in the early hours and swapped her car for the one registered to her at her home address. Ruth would return the next day to clean out any evidence of her career and make the move into retirement. Frank had agreed to dispose of the car and her weapons in his furnaces, a long-established route for anything metallic that was too dangerous to remain in circulation. Ruth even went to his yard to witness this final act. Frank and Ruth both raised a glass of fruit juice as the last 9mm pistol was melted.

On Monday, the head teacher at her school made a last attempt to encourage her to stay, but Ruth knew she hadn't the heart to stay. By the following Sunday she was flying south to a new life in Spain. She landed at around nine PM and was met at the airport by a hired driver, around mid-night she was in her village to be greeted by hugs and adoration of her elderly neighbours.
"How long are you staying for?" Asked Maria in her richly accented voice.
"Forever!" replied Ruth.

◆ ◆ ◆

NOTHING BETTER
TO DO.

The psychologist entered the uninspiring room in an uninspiring prison. That's how the system works, take away the inspiration, subjugate the person - order restored. The prisoner no-longer felt emotion, the system had removed that from his life. His life did not and could not matter to anyone. He was there to serve as a warning to others and a punishment to himself, he would die in prison without chance of redemption or rehabilitation. His life and position outside would not be restored, and he would not be rehabilitated.

"Thank you for agreeing to see me today." Enthused the dressed down young female who had entered the room. She offered a smile, it was not returned. Young and ambitious thought the terrorist, must be a postgrad looking to make a name for herself by researching the unrepentant.
"Don't thank me." Said the terrorist, addressing the wall from his chair. "You being here has already brightened my day."
"Thank you."

"Don't try that appeasement shit," the bitterness was evident in his voice. "I don't get visitors and seeing you is going to save me a couple of hours of lock up. Sit down" He gestured. "You can fuck off, I'm a pipe bomber, not a nonce." The terrorist snapped at the guard who remained in the uninspiring room, motionless. "If you're going to stay, at least make us a cup of tea!"

The terrorist told the psychologist how the nonce wing had got wind of the visit. They were dead jealous, the nonces couldn't understand why a political could be more interesting than child fiddlers and serial killers. Also, many would like the chance of updating their mental images for later gratification.

"I will be honest," she said. "Government funding, I get my research paid for if I can show a contribution to the PREVENT strategy."
"Well we better give them their monies worth. Screw, this will take ages, get a fucking tea organised and a chair if you're going to stay for my life-story."
The guard decided to make life easier for himself and made a call on the internal phone for an extra chair and three teas.
"Why were you attracted to terrorism?" Came the first question.
"Fuck me, the last one asked the very same." The terrorist wanted to cut the preliminaries. "You listen, record and take notes, I'll give you my version and we can do questions later. Okay?"
"Okay!"
"There are four kinds of people attracted to terror, those who haven't got a chance of stamping their will on the world – religious or political. They bomb and kill to raise their game, just occasionally they win. The romanticists who want adventure, to fight for a good cause – like old Byron, but it always goes wrong for them. Then there are those in it for the money or because they haven't got the security of a job and home, and of course there are the straight nut jobs who just want to kill."

"Which were you?"
"Needed the money. Building site work had dried up, twenty-eight and still living at home, girlfriend pregnant. It's not like you get offered a job. Just I'd been mouthing off about how shit life was

and who was to blame, then I get approached one night as I'm leaving our local club. My Da tried to pull me away, but it's like being touched by the devil. This guy told me everything I wanted to hear and offered me cash to take a package to a city. I did, even saved the ticket money by hitching a ride with a haulier. Being tight saved my life, the other guy they sent to do the same job was shot by the army ten minutes after he got off a bus. That was it, I had proved myself. I didn't show any remorse when my bomb went off in a shopping centre one Saturday afternoon, it killed kids, but I didn't care."

"What about your girlfriend and baby? Didn't that pip your conscious." The psychologist tried not to show some emotion.

"Couldn't give a fuck! She'd claimed it wasn't mine and moved to married quarters in Aldershot with a para. That was like a kick in the nuts. You know I once shot a para?"

"What?"

"Yeah, in cold blood." The terrorist grinned. "It was almost like a test, to see if I could be trusted for more frontline work. He was sat tied to a chair in a cesspit of an office in a disused factory. Our local leaders stood behind him as I was brought in, and his hood removed. That way he could see my face, he was sure to be killed. If I didn't do it then someone else would, as he knew my face and that could provide associations. Bastards really, I hate to think what happens to anyone who doesn't pull the trigger. The guy in charge of those operations was a psychologist just like you. Twisted fucker. I just walked up, picked up the gun and got on with it. The squaddie was pleading, but why prolong it. I did him a favour by getting it over with."

"Didn't you feel anything?"

"No, just got on with it. Fellas like me hardly have any remorse. We've been shat on from the day we were born. The movement gave me something back. A voice."

"I thought you were only in it for the money?"

"If that was true, I would have grassed and been out of here. A real

terrorist feels nothing for the victim. What is it you call it?"
"Empathy?"
"That's it. When you look out at people on the street, I suspect you see lives with meaning. Parents with children, careers, futures, marriages, homes and people with something to work for. I just see shapes passing by. Shapes who don't need to exist. Shapes that I may destroy in a few hours. Would their passing mean anything to me? No."

"Have you ever been tested for...."
"Fuck off!" Interrupted the terrorist. "I've been tested for every abnormality known, some say I'm just evil. No, I was just born in the wrong place and at the wrong time. I didn't have a career to work towards, an academic qualification or even the chance of building a business. Killing and maiming gave me the opportunity to be someone, gain a reputation. If you're really here to build profiles for PREVENT, just remember all the mentoring and programming won't help. The Asian lads here are the same, family had their life mapped out. Often marriage and work in a dead-end job or long hours in a family business. Little wonder racing around the desert in a pickup truck and beheading foreigners seemed more appealing. The most I could have hoped for was benefits, few hours cash-in-hand and council flat with a girl who despised me for getting her pregnant.

Blowing up shops, killing and kidnapping seemed vaguely glamorous. Also, I was given money to live off and expenses. Life as one of the big boys was good. People like some of my Da's friends even bought me drinks. They knew I wasn't away doing some driving job or fetching dodgy fags over the border. I was doing what they had read about at school, I was a volunteer. Most of them had been too young to have been involved in the early stuff and then too old to be of any use when it kicked off again. I was a hero."
"Are you still a hero?"

"Too right! Even in here I don't get half the shit other guys get. The nonces stay clear as they are likely to wind up dead if they try anything. Druggies leave you alone because there could be someone bigger and nastier than them on the outside who would gladly kill their family and destroy their businesses, the hard men just show respect and the Screws find it easier just not to give me any grief. And would you look at that, our tea has arrived. Thank you Jeeves!"

"Piss off!" Said the trustee delivering the tea. To prove his point the terrorist raised himself out of his seat and the teaboy hurried out before the terrorist was on his feet.
"Point proven?" Grinned the psychologist.

"Too right. That's what terror is all about, even for the nut jobs. We all just want recognition, to feel we've done something. Even if you don't approve, we have still done something that others haven't. I've been reading Byron. Why do you think a pounce like him wanted to go to Greece? Live off eating goats, shit in a ditch and get rogered by the Turks if he'd been captured? To help an oppressed people? He could have done that at home. He just wanted people to sit up and notice him, maybe possibly sell them a few books. If that meant wasting a few fuckers along the way, then so be it. But like all romantics, it went wrong."
"Did it go wrong for you?"
"Yes, I'm here!"
"Don't you have any regrets?" The psychologist felt the hollowness of his soul as she attempted eye contact.
"Yes, getting caught." Came the flippant reply.
"There were children who died in your last attack?" She was allowing her own emotions to intervene, she thought of her husband and the possibility of having to go through their first cycle of IVF.
"So what?"
"You don't regret killing innocents?"
"Innocents?" The psychologist felt she heard a slight anger in his

voice. "I gave immortality. Without me they would have grown up into a life of education, jobs, marriage and kids. Wage slaves to fund a corrupt economy and then die in obscurity. They now have their names on a memorial, they'll be remembered for ever. Isn't that what everyone wants? If you want to blame anyone, blame the government for not negotiating sooner, blame their parents for taking them shopping, the new great religion of consumerism or even blame them for being born. I don't see any use in the poor fuckers I wasted, what would any of them have achieved? That's the point of being a terrorist, the majority of us just want to destroy. Even when peace is declared there are still splinter groups and dissidents who carry on the fight. We'll say it's because our leaders have sold out, but really, we've just got nothing better to do."

"And that's why you murdered? Because there was nothing better to do?"

"Yes lady. You've hit the jackpot. There was nothing better to do. Even if I worked my arse off, I wouldn't get a job like yours. Yes, I can read a bit of poetry, but it came too late. Teaching English, I could have done that. But kids from where I come from didn't get to read poetry. So, with nothing better to do some of us went off to kill people."

"Anything else?"

"No, fuck it." The terrorist stared at the table. "Screw, my cell please."

The guard opened the door and two more officers escorted the terrorist out.

"You okay miss?" Asked the room guard.

"I think so." Answered the psychologist wiping away a tear.

"Hard bastard that one." Said the guard. "Will you be seeing him again?"

"No." She was definite in her answer. "I'll also make sure a transcript of this interview goes on his record, just in case anyone ever wants to fight for his parole."

Back in his cell the terrorist exchanged a few pleasantries with his fellow inmate with whom he'd been sharing for nearly a year.

"Everything okay?" Asked Chipolata - a fat gay chef with a small penis, who had become a kitchen trustee. Chipolata knew his acquired prison name could have been worse.

"Fantastic!" Came the unemotional reply. The terrorist and Chipolata would have been unlikely friends on the outside, but a stroke of administrative genius had brought them together. Chipolata would have been a ready victim, but the authorities knew no inmate would order the terrorist out of the cell while they bullied, assaulted and abused his cell mate. An inmate in another prison had attempted to place a drugs tax upon non-users and had crossed the terrorist's co-accused in doing so. The CSA now had one less claimant to sort out. Word had got around, and the terrorist and Chipolata were off limits. The authorities saw this as a work to be proud of, their most vulnerable inmate afforded protection by their most dangerous.

"Present." Said Chipolata handing the terrorist a bag of custard powder. "I don't get what you're doing with all them powders."
"Carbohydrates!" Came the response. "Flour, cornflour, custard powder and just about anything you can get."
"I've been asked to nick some weird shit out of the kitchen, but carbs?"
"You've never read about the great fire of London?"
"Only at school," Chipolata paused. "Didn't it start in a bakery?"
"Well done, you're learning, "grinned the terrorist. "Mix carbohydrates and air. Then add an ignition source and wait for the explosion. Blew the front of the Pudding Lane bakery clean out."
"You're not..."

The terrorist cut him short and told Chipolata not to worry as he wouldn't do anything until after the cook had completed his sentence later in the year.

"I've got it all in the air duct outside the governor's office, just stash a little more each time I'm sent up there to clean." He held up a short metal bar with a black plastic knob on the end." Took the lever off the control flap so no one can open it and knowing how long building services take to fix anything it'll be a long time before it's fixed."

Chipolata took a long look at the terrorist.

"Then what?"

"On a hot day when the fans are switched on, when I've nothing better to do I'll put the handle back on, open the flap and light a match."

BINARY

1925 Siberia

The political commissar looked down at the prisoner sat before him. They shivered together in a cold barren room illuminated by a solitary lightbulb that flickered in time to the spluttering generator in the building behind them. The commissar was unhappy at being dragged away from his evening vodka sat by an ailing wood stove, the only comforts in the last settlement of the Soviet Union that was still officially on land, beyond them lay only ice.

"Comrade," began the commissar sighing with despair, "this better be good, I could just hand you over to the OGPU and save myself the trouble of explaining why I still haven't had you shot."

"Because you need a telephone engineer?" came the prisoner's drawn out and muted reply. The commissar removed his hat and coat, he sat down and poured two glasses of balsam and vodka. The prisoner gratefully received the glass as the commissar lifted a sheet of grubby, uncared for paper:

"Explain?"

"It is source code," said the prisoner.

"We know it's code, that's why I was dragged out of the bar to conduct yet another pointless interrogation. One of your dreams?"

"A vision," replied the prisoner.

"You should drink more, it warms the blood and rots the brain; helps you accept what you are told."

This was the very reason the commissar had become a Bolshevik, he refused to accept what he had been told. It may have also been the reason for his posting to such a desolate place – it was colder than the hearts of the men that had sent him. As a hero of The Revolution, a sudden disappearance in Moscow would provoke suspicion. However, serving the cause and being lost in Siberia would leave an opening for a hero's funeral.

The two men stared at the walls and drank. The prisoner attempted to explain his handwritten notes.

"One day the world will unite, it will linked by cables, radios and machines beyond our belief. We will be able to send letters by typewriters that have screens with projected images. It will be like having a cinema on your desk. The code is a script to enable the machine to operate. It will have an electronic type of brain that needs instruction."

The commissar sat wondering, was this an idiot or a genius that he had before him. Having him shot would simplify his life in the tundra, but the potential for changing the world would be lost if he was a genius. If the prisoner was an idiot, it would have been simply cruel. For how less colourful the world would be without dreamers and fools.

"The code can be translated into binary, have you heard of that?"

The Commissar nodded a bored acceptance.

"All those numbers can be turned into an off or signal, something our limited technology can handle. The machines in the future will be able to translate it back into code and produce written text faster than any typist."

The prisoner explained his only problem was storing the code, storing it until the world managed to catch up with the vision he had of the world to come.

"This is all very well, but how will it aid the USSR?" asked the commissar looking for a reason to spare his prisoner.

"The USSR will no longer exist," the prisoner began to fear his own future, "but those who follow us will be able to use the system to infiltrate every institution in the world. One day we will even be able to ensure the results of the USA elections are at least favourable to Russia. Not by convincing voters, by altering the electronic files that will replace the paper versions."

The commissar reached for the bottle and then raised his glass in salute. Now he had a reason not to shoot the prisoner. He considered sending the idiot to Moscow to wind up his superiors. Sending him back to work on a secret project would also secure his own release from the kingdom of ice and snow. He thought the offer would be welcomed by the prisoner.

"No comrade," the prisoner looked forlorn, "I need to finish my work here first. Build the telephone exchange and store the code you have in your hand."

"Finish the exchange!" The commissar was shocked. "That could take years. Then the minute we leave the local savages will probably strip it for firewood."

"That's why once running, it will be sealed. The only contact it will have with the world will be a single cable coming from the ground."

The commissar was stunned, he knew the prisoner had dreams, it was thought he may have been epileptic, and the visions were some kind of brain disruption. However, even the best doctors in Moscow could not find any evidence of a brain disorder. Hence the prisoner was sent to build a telephone exchange in Siberia – to keep him away from others who would see him as a soothsayer or worse - a new hope. The commissar knew the accuracy of the prisoner's visions. He himself had won a month's salary by placing an illegal bet on the prediction of Lenin's death. The prisoner, although having no religious doctrine was able to predict the future with uncanny accuracy. It had been his prediction of the death of Trotsky that finally put him into conflict with the authorities.

On hearing rumours of his future death, Trotsky as head of the electro-technical board, and chairman of the scientific-technical board of industry; thought building a telephone exchange in Siberia a fitting punishment. The detail in the dreamers' predictions provided Trotsky with a troubled year in 1925 and further distanced him from the ruling elite in Moscow.

The telephone exchange would connect to the previously failed telegraph line, a line that an American company had attempted to run from Alaska to Moscow in the time of the Czar. A failed project that left the Soviets with a basic telegraph line that a Moscow planner thought might just be made to work.

The prisoner was a genius, and he was building an exchange that not only was able to give a basic voice service but could also store telegraph messages in a massive set of valves and diodes.These simple dots and dashes could then be transmitted when operators across the USSR had made the relevant connections. This had meant that time zones, repairs, connections, and prevailing weather could not interrupt a seamless system. It was a bold scheme and may have saved the prisoner's life when he revealed the vision at his trial. The Soviet judge laughed the scheme out of court and said the prisoner was either mad or a true visionary, so let him prove himself by building his vision.

However, the commissar wished he had not been the one sent to supervise the project. He was tasked with ensuring it at least reached a partial reality and provided the edges of the USSR with a working telephone network. He did console himself that he had not been sent to enforce farming targets as part of an impossible five-year plan.

The work continued, the miners dug the bunker, the engineers built a small power station that would run off the methane trapped under the tundra ice and the prisoner continued to dream. Dreams that would often become nightmares for the commissar who needed to explain away why his engineer needed to lie down in a darkened room and emerge with plans that appeared impossible to build. Plans that required the manufacture of parts that needed new techniques and stretched even the greatest Soviet engineers.

1989 Siberia

The alcohol driven clock in the centre of the bunker dripped one more drop of ethanol into the glass tube, it now had enough weight to begin a slow tilt. The mercury in the tube flowed and made the connection that would first switch on the gas heaters. Then when a working temperature had been reached the motors that had lain dormant for decades began to move. An auxiliary motor fired up and spun up to speed before it engaged the flywheel that would bring the complex to life. Within an hour a vast array of switches and relays would begin to click and transmit the modem noises that were so familiar to those going online in the latter part of the twentieth century.

"What the hell!" Screamed computer operators in Washington, Moscow and across Europe. Their superiors stared at the screens in disbelief as the message from beyond the realms of belief appeared before them.

"Fraternal greetings from the USSR. Wishing peace and goodwill to all citizens. Welcome to the world of the future. Comrade Dmitri Sokolov, Senior Telephone Engineer, Chukotsky District, Siberia, USSR. 9th November 1929."

Meanwhile in the geriatric ward of a Moscow hospital two old comrades raised glasses in salute to the world they had known and the new one they had helped to create.
"What are you two to celebrating?" asked their nurse.
"The New World of tomorrow that has started today," beamed the old commissar.
"Never," scoffed the nurse, "the world will never change."

The two old comrades just smiled as she served them their lunch. They were unaware of the convoy of Black Volga's that had stopped outside the hospital on that fateful day. They first became aware of the furore they had caused when boots were heard thudding on the hard hospital floors.

The nurse looked not in fear and loathing. But in admiration, the officer in plain clothes and his uniformed entourage formed a formidable presence. The uniforms saluted and the officer gave a small, dignified bow to the old gentlemen.

"What have they done now?" Asked the nurse.
The officer smiled. "It's what they did in the past, please have them bathed and dressed in their best clothes or uniforms. Whichever still fits" He quietly ordered. "And with any medals they may still have."

The nurse grunted showing indignity towards her charges. She was quickly reprimanded for her insolence. The officer, a KGB man to his core gave her a grave warning.
"They are wanted at the Kremlin. A dinner is planned in their honour. Have they spoken about what they did?"
The nurse nodded a no. She had heard conversations and was frightened to admit anything.

"Comrades!" Called the officer, turning to the old Bolsheviks as he left. "Any advice for the future?"

The dreamer closed his eyes and said.
"I will soon know Elysium. We are the sons and daughters who will unite in the starred galaxy."
"He's been mixing Beethoven and his medication." Joked the old commissar.

"Be wary of one an officer who is currently stationed in Dresden, he will hold the key to the future. He has the ability to put a new

Russia to the head of Europe and the world or destroy what we have all struggled to build. Please don't let him invade Ukraine."

The nurse made comments that it was definitely the medication. The KGB officer shook his head and took her aside. He knew of the events in happening in Berlin. He feared for his future and would need to take desperate measures to protect his interests. He did not understand why the Soviets would want to invade the Ukraine; it was part of the USSR. Did the dreamer really hold the key to the future? The old man would soon be 90 years old. How long had they left to access that unique mind? Or the fortune held in foreign banks on his behalf. It was the old man's genius and his friend's political knowledge that had kept them alive this long. The officer had reports from Siberia from the current Senior Telephone Engineer in Chukotsky who had joked that if there was a nuclear war, then he wanted to be in the bunker that the two old men had built. The cold even ensured the electrical parts did not overheat, always a challenge to electrical engineers.

The old comrades greatest success came when dreamer's vision of a woman in space had put the USSR years ahead in the space race. It was his friend the commissar, who manged to get the vision into the right ears and apply the much-needed persuasion to old deaf ears in the Kremlin. The USSR had women who were scientists, engineers, pilots, and adventurers. The USA had secretaries and housewives. They should strive for equality in space.

Valentina Tereshkova went into space in 1963 – 20 years ahead of the first US female astronaut. She remains the only woman to have been on a solo space mission. The success of the mission secured the two friends a commendation, increased salaries, and better accommodation for their families. It did not secure the fame and fortune they could have achieved in the west. However, they were respected and left to live their lives without the public glare and being turned out as a freaks on national television. A fate that has befallen one of the CIA's star psychic advisors.

The fortune came later. As the KGB knew, apart from his visions, the dreamer was a talented telephone engineer. Placed in a Berlin tunnel with a technical team at his disposal, he was able to intercept the majority of calls made by the US military and their primitive data transmissions. This also resulted in the pair encountering MI6, who wanted them to defect. The pair thought of their wives in Moscow and the warm beds that awaited their return.

However, they did form a lifelong friendship with an agent called O'Brian. He would place bets for them in Western betting shops based on the dreamer's visions. O'Brian was questioned by his own side and the CIA when he tried to collect on an outside bet predicting the date of the Kennedy assassination. The KGB were not happy about this either, as predicting the assassination of a US president implicated the USSR. Both sides reached the same conclusion - the dreamer had a gift. O'Brian agreed to cancel the rest of the accumulator bet he had placed against other Kennedy family members.

Since then, he kept the betting to venture capital and the dreamer predicting economic crashes. The only difficulty for his Russian friends was accessing their cash. O'Brian was honest, and after taking his cut; he invested their portion in the hope they would one day defect. There had been a number of clandestine meetings in East German toilets, where two identical suitcases were exchanged. One containing hard currency and the other potatoes – a personal joke between the three friends. The KGB and MI6 knew what was happening but were unwilling to interfere with an arrangement that could prove profitable to all sides. On the evening of the 9th of November 1989, the old friends were driven to the Kremlin to be received by members of the polit bureau.

Meanwhile in Dresden, a 37-year-old KGB officer witnessed the breakdown of communism. On the 5th December he faced a hostile crowd heading towards his headquarters. He felt lonelier than he ever had. The expected tanks were not coming to his aid.

"Don't try to force your way into this property. My comrades are armed, and they're authorised to use their weapons in an emergency." He shouted with an authority he didn't have. Days later he would begin the drive back to Leningrad with a second-hand washing machine, and years later he did go onto invade the Ukraine.

ABOUT THE AUTHOR

Ben Barker

Ben Barker is an English author living in the Midlands. A journalist and former teacher, he too has become a hidden person to protect his own identity and those close to him. While working in education, Ben had safeguarding responsibilities and was often drawn into protecting young people from the violent and sordid worlds that threaten them. Ben has an interest in the outdoors and this is often reflected in his writing.

He has previous written for local community publications and local press.

Printed in Great Britain
by Amazon